# Two Ways to Count to Ten

A Liberian Folktale | Retold by Ruby Dee
Illustrated by Susan Meddaugh

Henry Holt and Company · *New York*

Henry Holt and Company, LLC
*Publishers since 1866*
115 West 18th Street
New York, New York 10011

Henry Holt is a registered
trademark of Henry Holt and Company, LLC

Library of Congress Cataloging-in-Publication Data
Dee, Ruby.
Two ways to count to ten.
Summary: A retelling of a traditional African tale
in which King Leopard invites all the animals to a
spear-throwing contest whose winner will marry his
daughter and succeed him as king.
[1. Folklore—Africa.] I. Meddaugh, Susan, ill.
II. Title.
PZ8.1.D378Tw 1987 398.2'096 [E] 86-33513

ISBN 0-8050-1314-8
First published in hardcover in 1988 by Henry Holt and Company
First Owlet paperback edition—1990
Printed in Mexico

19  21  23  25  27  29  30  28  26  24  22  20  18

L̲ong, long ago, animals were not so different, one from the other. They were different colors, shapes, and sizes just as they are today, but they lived together in friendship and in peace. The leopard was king—rich beyond telling, mighty in his power and wisdom. All the animals respected and loved their king.

"Who shall I name to rule after me when I die?" King Leopard said one day to his beloved daughter. "I must seek out the cleverest beast in our jungle. I must find one who is wise enough to rule well. I shall make him a prince. Someday, my dear daughter, the two of you shall be queen and king."

King Leopard was pleased with his idea, and he planned a great feast. His royal drums carried the news of the feast far and wide throughout the jungle.

All the animals came as guests,
and they danced for three days.

At last the King told them to make a huge circle. Stepping into its center, he called his daughter to his side. Then he spoke in a loud voice.

"Listen, friends!" he cried. "Someday, when I am gone, another king must rule in my place. I will choose him now from among you so that he will be ready." There was a murmur of excitement all through the crowd.

"I shall seek the cleverest among you, for your king must be wise. He shall be a son to me and a husband to my dear daughter. He shall share all my riches."

Shouts came from the eager guests at the King's feast. No doubt each animal hoped that the good fortune would be his. Then King Leopard held up his hunting spear.

"Look at this, my people! Watch!" He flung the spear far up into the air and caught it when it fell to earth again. "With this spear, I will test you. He who would be our prince must also throw the spear toward the sky. He must send it so high that he can count to ten before it comes down again."

There was a buzz of talk among all the animals. This would not be so hard to do, they thought. One after another they came forward to try their skill. But first, each beast danced and sang before the King and his daughter.

"I will be first," said the elephant, pushing all the other beasts out of the way. The elephant danced clumsily. He was very big and his body was heavy. With his trunk in the air, he trumpeted all the fine deeds he would perform if he were king. "I will be king. I can do this thing!" he said. With his trunk, the great beast threw King Leopard's spear into the air.

"One! Two! Three!" he began counting.

But before the elephant had said "Four!," the King's spear dropped to the earth. The proud beast hung his head so low that the tip of his trunk dragged on the ground. He had failed.

Next came the bush ox. "I will be king. I can do this thing!" said the huge animal as he danced. "I'll throw the spear to the sun!" The bush ox picked up the spear in his mouth. With a mighty toss of his great head, he flung it far, far above his wide, gray horns.

"One! Two! Three! Four!" the bush ox counted. But he, too, was slow. Before he could say "Five!," the spear was down on the ground, and he went off, ashamed, into the jungle.

The chimpanzee was third. He jumped up and down, beating his hairy chest with his fists and singing of how much he would like to be king.

The chimpanzee rose up on his hind legs and held the spear in one hand, just like a man. "I will be king. I can do this thing!" he said. With a twist of his long arm, he threw it up toward the sky. "One-two-three-four-five-six-seven!" he chattered as fast as he could. The animals held their breath. Surely, with such a quick tongue he would make the count.

But he did not! Just as he said "Eight!" the spear fell into his hand.

Then the crowd parted as the lion stepped majestically into the center of the circle. The lion had always wanted to be king anyway, and now was his chance to prove that *he* was the finest animal in the jungle. With a fling of his mighty mane, he danced and sang of his royal intentions. "*I* will be king. I can do this thing!" he sang.

And as the other animals looked on in awe, the lion twirled his tail around the spear and threw it skyward with a thunderous roar. "One! Two! Three! Four!" The spear rose higher and higher. "Five! Six! Seven! Eight! Nine!"

Just as he said "Nine!" the spear pierced the earth at his feet. The lion was furious. Off he stomped into the bushes.

One by one the other animals tried to count to ten while the spear was still in the air. One by one they all failed.

"It seems I must look somewhere else for a beast who is clever enough to rule when I am gone," King Leopard said sadly.

"Let me try to throw your spear, O King," came a brave voice from the crowd and out stepped the slender antelope. "I would like to marry your beautiful daughter. I will be king. I can do this thing!"

"Ho! Ho! Ho! Hah! Hah! Hah!" The other animals broke into laughter. How could this weak and puny creature possibly throw the King's spear high enough to count to more than two or three? How could he hope to succeed where all the other animals—even the lion—had failed?

But the young antelope would not be turned aside. "I wish to try," he insisted. King Leopard nodded his head.

"Who can say what any creature can do until he has tried?" The King said to the crowd. "The antelope may throw the spear."

So, the other animals moved back to give him room. When the antelope danced, King Leopard's daughter was very pleased. No one could deny that his steps were more graceful than all the other animals' steps.

With a toss of his head, he flung the spear far up into the air. Before it could fall to earth, he called out five words.

"Two! Four! Six! Eight! Ten!" he cried. "I have counted to ten. King Leopard did not say how the count was to be made."

The King laughed and nodded his royal head. "No, I did not say how the count was to be made," he agreed. "And as everyone knows, one can count to ten by twos as well as by ones. Remember, my friends, it is not always the biggest or the strongest, but sometimes the cleverest that wins the prize. The antelope has won the contest. He shall be king."

At the wedding feast which King Leopard gave for his daughter, the animals all cheered their clever new prince.

# THE ILLUSTRATED HISTORY OF WORLD WAR II

*Owen Booth*
*and*
*John Walton*

CHARTWELL
BOOKS, INC.

**CHARTWELL BOOKS, INC.**
A Division of
**BOOK SALES, INC.**
114 Northfield Avenue
Edison, New Jersey 08837

ISBN 0-7858-1016-1

Editorial and design by
Brown Packaging Books Ltd
Bradley's Close
74–77 White Lion Street
London N1 9PF


Printed in Singapore

Project Editor: Brian Burns
Editor: Brenda Ralph Lewis
Design: wda
Picture research: Adrian Bentley